# BULLDOZER Dreams

by Sharon Chriscoe

illustrated by
John Joven

RP|KIDS
PHILADELPHIA

Running Press Kids
Hachette Book Group
1290 Avenue of the Americas, New York, NY 10104
www.runningpress.com/rpkids
@RP_Kids

Printed in Canada

First Edition: October 2017

Published by Running Press Kids, an imprint of Perseus Books, LLC,
a subsidiary of Hachette Book Group, Inc.

The Hachette Speakers Bureau provides a wide range of authors for
speaking events. To find out more, go to www.hachettespeakersbureau.com
or call (866) 376-6591.

The publisher is not responsible for websites (or their content)
that are not owned by the publisher.

Print book cover and interior design by T.L. Bonaddio

Library of Congress Control Number: 2016945291

ISBNs: 978-0-7624-5966-7 (hardcover); 978-0-7624-6202-5 (ebook);
978-0-7624-6423-4 (ebook); 978-0-7624-6424-1 (ebook)

1010

10 9 8 7 6 5 4 3 2

**TO RICKY II, CHERYLENNA, AND RICHIE:**

*May all your dreams come true.*

*Love, Mom*

**TO GOD:**

*For giving me every single dream in my life.*
*—J. J.*

The clearing is done.
The sun disappears.

A bulldozer stops. He shifts down his gears.

He surveys his site. No hills, bumps, or trees.

He's leveled the mounds of dirt with great ease.

He looks to his left.

And then to his right.

It's time to go home.

He's done for the night.

He lifts up his blade.
His spotlights flash on.
He rolls through the gate and
lets out a yawn.

# WIGGLE and SHAKE

He heads to the wash. He stretches his track.

He scrubs and he cleans—every crevice and crack.

He wiggles and shakes. He exits the bay.

All polished and shined,
his tummy gives way . . .

. . . to rumbles and growls.
It's time for a fill.

He punches his clutch and climbs up the hill.

He pulls in the station, sipping each slurp.

His belly pan swells, and up comes a burp.

He nuzzles his cone. He nestles in tight.

He chooses a book to read for the night.

A push and a shove to smooth out the land.
He burrows his tracks down deep in the sand.

The heat from the day is cooled by the night.
He closes his cab and turns off his light.
The little stars dance down low in the sky.
The moon casts its light as shadows pass by.

His axles relax.
His cylinders steam.
His engine purrs softly.

zzzZZZZ

He drifts to a dream.

He lowers his blade. He turns on his track.
A puff of black smoke comes out of his stack.
He revs up his motor, pushing through rocks.
He scoops them up high and stacks them like blocks.

He makes one last pass. He toots on his horn.
The children arrive. A playground is born.
They swing and they slide. They race and have fun.

Loud cheers fill his dream.
His work here is done.